BILLY
The
Littlest One

by
MIRIAM SCHLEIN

pictures by
Lucy Hawkinson

Albert Whitman & Company
Chicago

What is it like to be little?
I know.

Because I am the littlest one.

When I look out
of the window,
the window sill is up
to my nose.

I can never go
anywhere alone.
Someone's always
following me.

I am always
the first one
to go to sleep at night,
but that's all right.

Because I'm
the first one up
in the morning!

The littlest one is always
first.
That's how it seems to me.

Except when we go someplace.
Then I always seem to get
there last.

That's how it is, when you're
the littlest one.

But I'm not the only littlest one.

No.

Once we went to the zoo.

Of all the elephants,

there was a littlest one, too.

I liked him best.

He was so little

he could stand right under

his mother.

But he was not
the only littlest one.

I saw the littlest monkey.
He was drinking milk
from a bottle.

There was a littlest bear.

He was climbing on the rocks,

the way I like to do.

How are things,
when you're the littlest one?

Things are just right.

I have a spoon and fork
just right for me.

I have a little room
just right for me.

I have a little chair
just right for me.

And a little bed
just right for me.

Will I always
be the
littlest one?

Oh, no.

Not me.

Because I keep getting bigger!

Some day
a new little one
may come walking
down the street.

And then I won't be
the littlest one
any more!